A l   nce

Scripture taken from the Common English Bible ®, CEB® Copyright © 2010, 2011 by Common English Bible. ™
Used by permission. All rights reserved worldwide. The "CEB" and "Common English Bible" trademarks are
registered in the United States Patent and Trademark Office by Common English Bible. Use of either trademark
requires the permission of Common English Bible.

ISBN: 1541077032
ISBN-13: 978-1541077034

DEDICATION

This book is dedicated to all of the Kingdom Warriors in this world. We all have a part to play, and however small it seems to be we are working towards the same ultimate goal.

1 Corinthians 12:4-11

Glory to God, who is able to do far beyond all that we could ask or imagine by his power at work within us.

Ephesians 3:20

ACKNOWLEDGMENTS

I would first like to thank my husband, Joe, without whom any of this would be possible. I am truly blessed to have you in my life. Thank you, Coco, for all of your help. Thank you to my HSS and friends, who offered encouragement on this venture. I would also like to thank my instructor, Keith Yates, for starting me on the path that led to where I am now. If you had not invested in my martial arts training, none of this would have come to fruition.

I am incredibly grateful for all of you.

Karate class was over at DMD Martial Arts, and the dojo was abuzz with the sounds of eager students rushing out to greet their parents. There were excited yells and scurrying noises, seemingly coming from every direction.

The floor was littered with forgotten sparring gear, shoes, and bags. The instructor slowly walked back and forth, picking up the items and calling out to their owners.

"Cathy, don't forget your water bottle!"
"Ryan, you dropped your mouthpiece case." he said, handing it to his senior student.

"Thank you!" Ryan stammered, throwing it in his bag hurriedly.

"Bye Sensei!" called out Elizabeth as she darted out the door. The instructor raised his hand to wave goodbye as the door thumped shut. The noise level began to die down.

Soon enough the dojo was almost completely empty, save for a bag of gear in the lobby area and one remaining student. As the teacher walked in that direction, he recognized who still remained.

David, one of his youngest students, sat on the wooden bench. He looked troubled.

Sensei sat down beside David. He knew what was bothering him right away, but still he asked.

"David, why are you sitting here all by yourself?" Briefly, the instructor reflected on how far David had come since beginning class at DMD Martial Arts. David was such a hard-working student and truly had a heart of gold, but he had to work very hard to attain the same ranks that came easily to many of his other students.

There was a long pause before David let out a quiet sigh. "Sir, I'm not any good. It seems like everyone is better than me."

"Why would you say that, David?" the teacher replied calmly.

"They all learn faster! They get new belts faster! I try so hard, but I just don't think I'm good!" David looked as though he were near tears.

"Are you saying you want to give up, David?" the man asked.

There was another pause, then David replied, "No, I don't. I won't. But it's so hard!"

"I'm very glad you want to keep working." Sensei smiled. "David, do you know what perseverance means?"

"You say it in class all the time; it means not giving up."

"Very good, that's true," Sensei answered. "But more important than what the dictionary says about perseverance is what I have learned from my Master."

Each person should test their own work and be happy with doing a good job and not compare themselves with others. Each person will have to carry their own load. Those who are taught the word should share all good things with their teacher, make no mistake, God is not mocked. A person will harvest what they plant.

Those who plant only for their own benefit will harvest devastation from their selfishness, but those who plant for the benefit of the spirit will harvest eternal life from the spirit.

Galatians 6:9 - Let's not get tired of doing good, because in time we'll have a harvest if we don't give up.

So then, let's work for the good

David looked inquisitively at his teacher, awaiting his words.

"Let's not get tired of doing good, because in time we'll have a harvest if we don't give up."

David's eyes lit up briefly. "I've heard that before, I think...." he trailed. "But I can't remember where."

"It's in Galatians 6:9," replied Sensei.

"Ga-lay-shens?" David said with a puzzled look on his face. "Sir, who *was* your instructor? Who taught *you?*"

"God", Sensei replied quietly, then smiled gently.

There was a long silence, save for a very slight echo following the teacher's last word.

David pondered his teacher's words, as a smile slowly came to his face. "That verse is from the Bible, isn't it?!"

"Yes, David, it is. Did you know in the Bible, there is a story of a good man named Daniel, who was taken from his home in Jerusalem? He was made to work in the service of King Nebuchadnezzar in Babylon for years!"

David's eyes grew wide. He loved stories!

"Daniel had great faith in God, and though the city around him commanded he change his identity and lifestyle, he persevered through many difficult years. He wouldn't let his circumstances change his resolve to do what was right - even when his life was threatened many times. In fact, he was even thrown into a den of hungry lions at one point! Do you know how scary, and how hard that must have been for him?"

David shook his head and looked down, thinking how Daniel's hardships must have been much greater than his own. It seemed silly to worry about karate class, when others have truly had trials he didn't understand.

Sensei continued, "Not only did Daniel persevere, but he had indomitable spirit."

"We learned that in class, too!" David exclaimed.

"Yes, we did. And I'll tell you a good story about that another time. You see, David, Daniel's perseverance gave him something much more important than belts or trophies."

"What's that?" David asked.

"His rewards were greater than anything you could gain on this earth. His treasures were in Heaven. David, let me tell you something important before you go. In life, talent comes and goes, but true perseverance will lead you anywhere your heart wishes to go. But we cannot lean on our own strength, we must learn to rely on the strength of our one true Master."

Just then, David heard the honk of his mom's car outside. He jumped up, grabbing his things to go. He just realized they were the only ones left in the quiet dojo.

He paused for a moment, unsure of what to say. "Thank you, sir."

"You are most welcome."

"But... what happened to Daniel and the hungry lions?" he asked worriedly.

"God closed up their mouths," Sensei said with a grin. "You can read about it in Daniel 6:16-24 with your parents."

David's eyes grew wide again as he smiled ear to ear. And with that, he rushed out the door.

Many years later, David's teacher went on an exciting trip across town. He slowly walked up to a building with a sign freshly painted on the door.

"Kingdom Warrior Martial Arts"

He peered in the window, only to see David, a grown man, inside. He proudly smiled at how far his former student had come.

As he reached for the door handle, he saw David kneel down in front of one of his students. The student seemed upset, and was sitting on the floor. Sensei smiled as he watched David take a seat next to him and begin talking.

"This visit can wait," whispered Sensei. "Great work is being done here." Then he turned his face to the blue sky above and whispered,
"Thank You."

Glossary of Japanese Martial Arts Terms

Do – The Way

Dojo – Karate School

Domo Arigato – Many Thanks

Gi – Uniform

Hai – Yes

Hajime – "Begin" Command

Karate-Do – Way of Empty Hand

Karate-ka – Student

Kata – Forms

Oss – Respectful Greeting (alternatively "osu", but commonly used as oss to depict pronunciation)

Rei – Bow

Senpai – Senior Belt

Sensei – Literally, "the one who has gone before." Commonly used to mean Teacher

Seiretsu – Line Up

Seiza – Sitting at Attention

Yame – "Stop" Command

Counting to 10 in Japanese:
Ichi

Ni

San

Shi

Go

Roku

Shichi

Hachi

Ku

Ju

For exclusive Parent/Instructor bonus content, please visit www.dmdtaekwondo.com

ABOUT THE AUTHOR

Ginny Aversa Tyler is a wife and homeschooling mother of three children.
She is the owner and founder of DMD Tae Kwon Do, a Christian martial arts school near
McKinney, Texas. (www.dmdtaekwondo.com)

Inspired by the endless lessons both God's Word and the martial arts have to offer, Ginny
created the Kingdom Kicks book series for children so that they may tie their love of the
martial arts to the lifelong guidance our Heavenly Father has offered.

Ginny's passion for teaching, not just her own children and students, is the basis for the
Kingdom Kicks series, through which she wishes to inspire children all over the world to seek
Biblical truths outside the walls of their home, school, and martial arts classes.

47603392R00027

Made in the USA
San Bernardino, CA
03 April 2017